the
lonesome
puppy

the lonesome puppy

Y O S H I T O M O   N A R A

chronicle books · san francisco

I was all alone
and lonesome.

I was always hoping
for someone, somewhere,
to be my friend.

It's true. I was all alone,
and this is why.

I am . . .

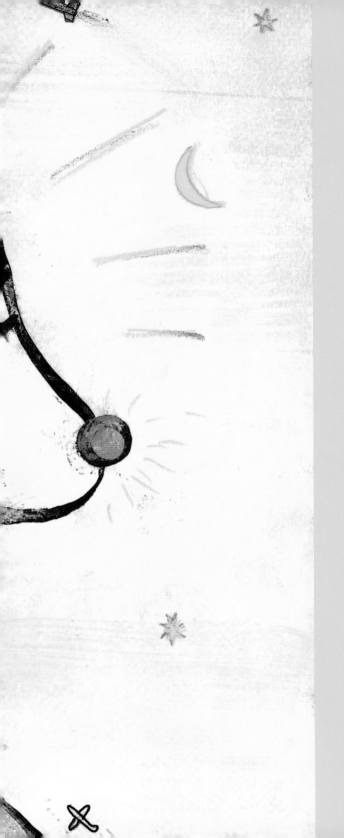

...this BIG!

I was too big
for anyone to notice me,
and that is why
I was always
all alone and lonesome.

But then,
one day...

She
climbed
and
climbed.

And climbed
some more.

And walked, and walked, until finally

she arrived at my head.

When she got to the top of my head
she slipped and fell and tumbled—CRASH!

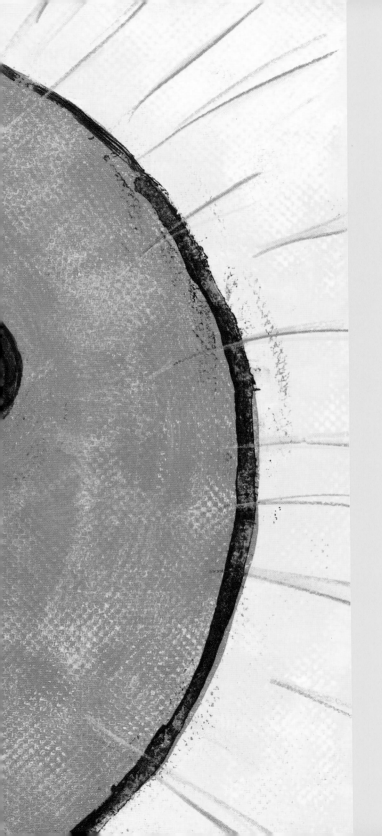

The girl was very surprised.

I was surprised, too.

But then the girl sang songs for me,
and we became friends.

I took the girl home.

"See you again!!" she said.

Now I am not lonesome any more.

The little girl and the big puppy
each found a friend.

And they were friends forever.
Though sometimes they fought,
as friends do,
they still had fun and played together.

No matter how alone you are,
there is always someone,
somewhere, waiting to meet you.

Just look and you will find them!

First published in the United States in 2008 by Chronicle Books LLC.

Copyright © 1999 by Yoshitomo Nara.
Translation © 2008 by Chronicle Books LLC.
Originally published in Japan in 1999 by Magazine House.
All rights reserved.

Tomio Koyama Gallery
Hakutosha
Moichi Kuwabara
Yutaka Tosa

English language translation by Tomoko Fujii.
English type design by Sara Gillingham.
Typeset in Regular Joe.
Manufactured in China.

Library of Congress Cataloging-in-Publication Data
Nara, Yoshitomo, 1959-
The lonesome puppy / Yoshitomo Nara.
p. cm.
Summary: A puppy so large that no one notices him is very lonely
until he meets a determined little girl.
ISBN: 978-0-8118-5640-9
[1. Dogs—Fiction. 2. Friendship—Fiction.]   I. Title.
PZ7.N156Lo 2008
[E]—dc22
2006006754

10 9 8 7 6 5 4 3 2 1

Chronicle Books LLC
680 Second Street, San Francisco, California 94107

www.chroniclekids.com